Read to Me, Daddy

Introduction and compilation
Copyright © 1995 by Random House Value Publishing, Inc.
All rights reserved

This edition is published by JellyBean Press,
distributed by
Random House Value Publishing, Inc.
40 Engelhard Avenue
Avenel, New Jersey 07001

Random House
New York • Toronto • London • Sydney • Auckland

Cover painting by Gary Overacre

Printed and bound in the United States of America

Library of Congress Cataloging-in-Publication Data
Read to me, daddy.
p. cm.
Summary: A collection including poems and such traditional stories as
"Chicken Licken," "The Little Red Hen," and "Little Tuppens."
1. Tales. 2. Children's poetry. [1. Folklore. 2. Poetry—Collections.]
PZ5.R19842 1995
808.8'99282—dc20
94-39814
CIP
AC

ISBN 0-517-12327-4

8 7 6 5 4 3 2 1

Read to Me, Daddy

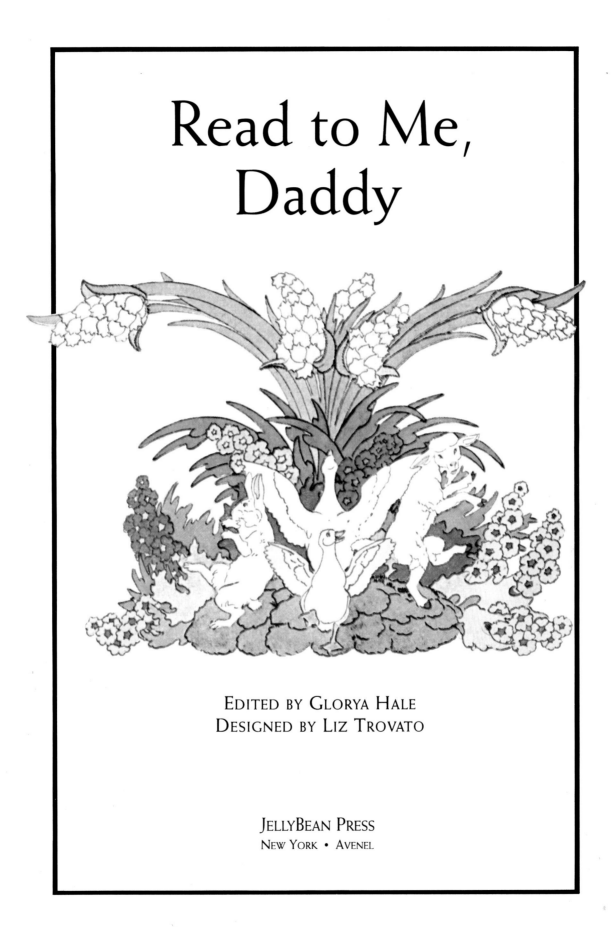

EDITED BY GLORYA HALE
DESIGNED BY LIZ TROVATO

JELLYBEAN PRESS
NEW YORK • AVENEL

CONTENTS

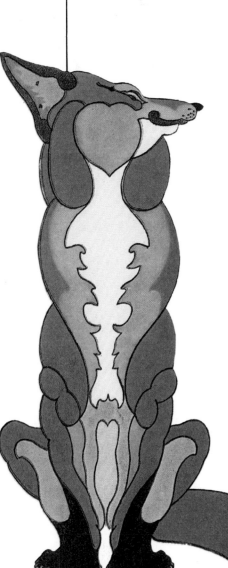

INTRODUCTION

"Once upon a time . . . ." The very words may awaken in you, as they do in many grown-ups, memories of childhood, of the pleasures of nestling close to your father and feeling the deep resonance of his voice as you listened to him read his favorite poems and the magical stories that have been told and retold since the days when storytelling began.

In this book you will again meet the three bears who are so upset when a little blond intruder disturbs their neat house in the forest, and Chicken Licken, who manages to convince her friends that the sky is falling. Here, too, is the gingerbread boy who runs away from the little old woman who baked him, and the industrious little red hen who teaches a lesson to her lazy neighbors.

There are, also, verses by Edward Lear, including the ridiculous tale of "The Pobble Who Has No Toes," selections from Elizabeth Gordon's delightful *Bird Children*, and memorable poems by Robert Louis Stevenson, Eugene Field, and Christina Rossetti. The evocative illustrations were done by such well-known artists as Frederick Richardson, Jessie Willcox Smith, and Margaret W. Tarrant.

This is a wonderful collection of stories of long, long ago, when animals talked, and frequently made a lot of sense, of hilarious nonsense verse, and much-loved poems. It is a book that you will find a pleasure to share with the child who asks, "Please read to me, Daddy."

GLORYA HALE

The THREE BEARS

In a far-off country, long, long ago, there lived a little girl who was called Goldilocks because of her beautiful golden curls.

Goldilocks loved to walk through the woods gathering wildflowers and to run through the open fields chasing butterflies. Sometimes she would sit quietly at the edge of a pond and watch the frogs jumping in and out of the water.

One day she was picking flowers and walked farther into the woods than she had ever been before. It seemed rather strange and lonely there. Then she saw a snug little house in which three bears lived. One was great big Papa Bear, one was medium-sized Mama Bear, and the third was wee little Baby Bear. Of course, Goldilocks did not know that three bears lived there.

The door of the little house was open. Goldilocks peeped in and saw that it was empty. She knocked on the door. Nobody answered. Since no one was home she stepped inside to look around a bit.

The three bears had just gone out for a walk and they had left their three bowls of porridge on the table to cool.

Goldilocks was very hungry after her long walk and the porridge smelled so good. She thought that she would like just a taste of it. First she tasted the porridge in the great big bowl, which belonged to Papa Bear, but it was too hot.

Next she tasted the porridge in the medium-sized bowl, which belonged to Mama Bear, but it was too cold.

Then she tasted the porridge in the little bowl, which belonged to Baby Bear. This porridge was just right. She took one spoonful and then another. Before she knew it, she had eaten it all.

Now that she was no longer hungry, Goldilocks looked around the room. She saw that there were three chairs. She climbed up into the great big chair, which belonged to Papa Bear, but it was much too high.

Then she climbed into Mama Bear's medium-sized chair, but it was much too wide.

Finally, she sat down in Baby Bear's little chair and it was just right. She sat in the chair for a few minutes, very pleased that it was so comfortable.

Suddenly, she heard a creak and a crunch. Then the chair broke and she fell to the floor.

Goldilocks picked herself up and brushed herself off. I'm very tired, she thought. Maybe I can have a little nap. She went into another room where she saw three beds. She climbed up into Papa Bear's great big bed, but it was much too hard.

Next she tried Mama Bear's medium-sized bed, but it was much too soft.

Finally, she lay down on Baby Bear's little bed, which was very comfortable. She snuggled under the covers and fell fast asleep.

While Goldilocks was sleeping, the three bears came home from their walk and went quickly to the table to eat their porridge.

Papa Bear looked down at his bowl and said in his great big voice, "SOMEBODY HAS BEEN TASTING MY PORRIDGE!"

Then Mama Bear looked into her bowl and said in her medium-sized voice, "SOMEBODY HAS BEEN TASTING MY PORRIDGE!"

And then Baby Bear looked into his bowl and piped up in his little voice, *"Somebody has been tasting my porridge, and has eaten it all up!"*

Then they looked at their chairs. Papa Bear saw that the cushion from his chair was on the floor. "SOMEBODY HAS BEEN SITTING IN MY CHAIR!" he roared.

And Mama Bear saw that the cushion on her chair was pushed to one side. "SOMEBODY HAS BEEN SITTING IN MY CHAIR!" she said.

And then Baby Bear saw his chair and cried, *"Somebody has been sitting in my chair and has broken it all to pieces!"*

The bears knew that someone had come into their house and, perhaps, was

still there. They tiptoed as quietly as they could into their bedroom. Papa Bear saw that his pillow was on the floor. "SOMEBODY HAS BEEN LYING IN MY BED!" he said in a loud voice, completely forgetting that the stranger might still be in the house.

Then Mama Bear noticed that the quilt, which had been neatly covering her bed, was now all mussed up. "SOMEBODY HAS BEEN LYING IN MY BED!" she said in a loud whisper.

And then Baby Bear cried, *"Somebody has been lying in my bed, and here she is!"*

The three bears stared in great astonishment at the pretty little girl with the golden hair who was fast asleep in Baby Bear's bed.

Suddenly, Goldilocks woke up. She saw the three bears and was so frightened that she jumped out of bed, then ran quickly past them into the next room and out the front door. She ran through the woods as fast as her legs could carry her, and she never again went near the snug little house that was deep in the woods.

As for the three bears, while Mama Bear made some more porridge, Papa Bear repaired Baby Bear's chair. Then they all sat down and ate their porridge.

The Man They Made

We made a man all by ourselves;
    We made him jolly fat;
We stuck a pipe into his face,
    And on his head a hat.

We made him stand upon one leg,
    So that he might not walk,
We made his mouth without a tongue,
    So that he might not talk.

We left him grinning on the lawn
    So we to bed might go;
But in the night he ran away,
    Leaving a heap of snow!

HAMISH HENDRY

Block City

What are you able to build with your blocks?
Castles and palaces, temples and docks.
Rain may keep raining, and others go roam,
But I can be happy and building at home.

Let the sofa be mountains, the carpet be sea,
There I'll establish a city for me:
A church and a mill and a palace beside,
And a harbor as well where my vessels may ride.

Great is the palace with pillar and wall,
A sort of a tower on the top of it all,
And steps coming down in an orderly way
To where my toy vessels lie safe in the bay.

This one is sailing and that one is moored:
Hark to the song of the sailors on board!
And see, on the steps of my palace, the kings
Coming and going with presents and things!

Now I have done with it, down let it go!
All in a moment the town is laid low.
Block upon block lying scattered and free,
What is there left of my town by the sea?

Yet as I saw it, I see it again,
The church and the palace, the ships and the men,
And as long as I live and where'er I may be,
I'll always remember my town by the sea.

ROBERT LOUIS STEVENSON

Winter

Bread and milk for breakfast,
And woolen frocks to wear,
And a crumb for robin redbreast
On the cold days of the year.

CHRISTINA ROSSETTI

The LITTLE RED HEN

ne day long, long ago, a little red hen was scratching around in the farmyard and found a nice, round grain of wheat.

"This wheat should be planted," she said. "Who will plant this grain of wheat?"

"Not I," quacked the duck.

"Not I," meowed the cat.

"Not I," barked the dog.

"Then I will just have to plant it myself," said the little red hen. And she did. Soon the wheat came up and before long it grew to be tall and golden. It was ready to be cut.

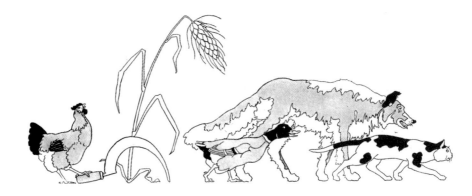

"The wheat is ripe," said the little red hen. "Who will help me harvest it?"

"Not I," quacked the duck.

"Not I," meowed the cat.

"Not I," barked the dog.

"Well, then I will just have to harvest this ripe golden wheat myself," said the little red hen. And she did.

When the wheat was harvested, the grain had to be taken from the husk. "Who will help me thresh this wheat?" the little red hen asked.

"Not I," quacked the duck.

"Not I," meowed the cat.

"Not I," barked the dog.

"Well, I guess I will just have to thresh the wheat myself," said the little red hen. And she did.

When the wheat was all threshed, it had to be taken to the mill so the grain could be ground into flour. "Who will help me take this wheat to the mill?" asked the little red hen.

"Not I," quacked the duck.

"Not I," meowed the cat.

"Not I," barked the dog.

"Well," said the little red hen, "I'll just have to carry this heavy bag of grain to the mill myself." And she did.

After the grain had been ground into flour and the little red hen had carried the bag of flour back to the farmyard, she asked, "Who will help me make a loaf of bread from this fine flour?"

"Not I," quacked the duck.

"Not I," meowed the cat.

"Not I," barked the dog.

"Then I will just have to make this bread myself," said the little red hen. And she did.

When the bread was baked, the little red hen took the loaf out of the oven. It smelled marvelous. "Now who will help me eat this delicious fresh bread?" asked the little red hen.

"Oh! I will," quacked the duck.

"And I will, too," meowed the cat.

"And I certainly will," barked the dog.

"No, no you won't!" said the little red hen. "I got no help from any of you when I planted the grain of wheat, harvested the wheat when it grew tall and golden, threshed the grain, carried the grain to the mill to have it ground into flour, carried the flour back to the farmyard, and then baked this lovely loaf of bread. Now I am going to eat all of it myself." And she did.

BIRD CHILDREN

Sir Rooster is a noisy chap,
He wakes you from your morning nap.
He sleeps but little all night through,
Crows at eleven, one, and two.

Dear little downy Gosling said,
"I can't get learning through my head;
I really don't see what's the use—
When I grow up I'll be a goose."

Said Father Goose, "I think I'll take
A stroll this morning to the lake."
Mother Goose said, "Then I'll go, too,
And maybe take a swim with you."

Said Yellow Duckling to his brother,
"Come on, let's hide away from Mother,"
But he replied, "Oh, dear me, no!
We'd better not, she'd worry so."

Madam Swan's a graceful lady,
Likes to float where banks are shady;
When Father Swan goes out to swim
He takes the cygnets out with him.

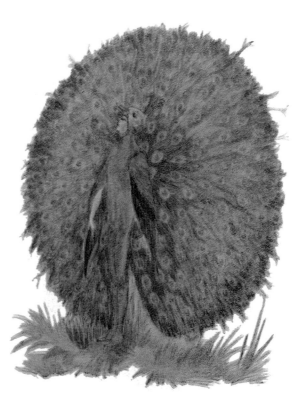

Peacock's a bird of much renown
And wears a lovely cap and gown;
They say he's very, very vain
And likes to show his sweeping train.

Friendly little Chickadee
Is just as cunning as can be;
Upon your windowsill he'll come
And thank you kindly for a crumb.

Cardinal Bird wears vivid red,
He's very amiable, 'tis said;
He likes fresh fruit and seeds to eat
And has a song that's very sweet.

Eagle has piercing yellow eyes,
He's very strong and very wise.
He's king and master over all
The other birds, both great and small.

Little Sir Screech Owl and his wife
Live such a cheerful, useful life.
They nest among the apple trees,
Saying, "May we eat the bugs here, please?"

Said Penguin, pensively, one day,
"Come, fishie dear, come out and play,"
But fishie answered, in a fright,
"I've heard about your appetite."

31

Albatross has wings so strong
That he could fly the whole day long.
But if he's tired, he can float
Upon the waves, just like a boat.

The dainty Misses Parakeet
Dress all in green and look so sweet.
From South America they came
And "Love Bird" is their other name.

Hummingbird, the dainty thing,
Has no voice and cannot sing,
He flies quickly, and he sips
Honey from the flowers' lips.

Sandpiper lives beside the water
With her little son and daughter.
She shows the cunning little brood
Exactly where to look for food.

Parrot's a very wise old bird,
She can speak English well, I've heard;
Laughs and says in a manner jolly,
"Have you a cracker for Miss Polly?"

Ivory-Billed Woodpecker said, "Dear me!
They're cutting down my family tree;
Where can I live, I'd like to know,
If men will spoil the forest so?"

Here is old Mr. Pelican,
He is a famous fisherman;
Said he, "I do not mind wet feet
If I catch fish enough to eat."
ELIZABETH GORDON

Pirate Story

Three of us afloat in the meadow by the swing,
Three of us aboard in the basket on the lea.
Winds are in the air, they are blowing in the spring,
And waves are on the meadow like the waves there are at sea.

Where shall we adventure, today that we're afloat,
Wary of the weather and steering by a star?
Shall it be to Africa, a-steering of the boat,
To Providence, or Babylon, or off to Malabar?

Hi! but here's a squadron a-rowing on the sea—
Cattle on the meadow a-charging with a roar!
Quick, and we'll escape them, they're as mad as they can be,
The wicket is the harbor and the garden is the shore.

ROBERT LOUIS STEVENSON

Foreign Lands

Up into the cherry tree
Who should climb but little me?
I held the trunk with both my hands
And looked abroad on foreign lands.

I saw the next door garden lie,
Adorned with flowers, before my eye,
And many pleasant places more
That I had never seen before.

I saw the dimpling river pass
And be the sky's blue looking-glass;
The dusty roads go up and down
With people tramping into town.

If I could find a higher tree
Farther and farther I should see,
To where the grownup river slips
Into the sea among the ships.

To where the roads on either hand
Lead onward into fairy land,
Where all the children dine at five,
And all the playthings come alive.

ROBERT LOUIS STEVENSON

The HOUSE ON THE HILL

nce upon a time, there was a curly-tailed pig who lived on a farm. He had many friends and the food was plentiful and very good. But he was tired of living in a muddy pen.

One day he said to his friend the sheep: "I am tired of living in a muddy pen. I am going to build myself a house on the hillside."

"Baa, Baa! I'm tired of living here, too. May I go with you?"

"What can you do to help?" asked the pig.

"I can haul the logs for the house," said the sheep.

"Oink, oink! That would certainly be a help," said the pig. "Please do come with me."

As the pig and the sheep walked through the farmyard and talked about their new house, they met their friend the goose.

"Good morning," said the goose. "Where are you both going this beautiful sunny morning?"

"We are going to build ourselves a house on the hillside. We are tired of living here," said the pig.

"Quack, quack!" said the goose. "I am tired of living here, too. I would like to live in a nice house. May I go with you?"

"What can you do to help?" asked the pig.

"I can gather moss, and stuff it into the cracks to keep out the rain."

"Oink, oink!" said the pig.

"Baa, baa!" said the sheep.

"That would certainly be a help," said the pig. "Please do come with us."

As the pig and the sheep and the goose walked out of the farmyard and talked about their new house, they met a rabbit.

"Good morning, rabbit," said the pig.

"Good morning," said the rabbit. "Where are you going this fine morning?"

"We are going to the hillside to build a house for ourselves. We are tired of living on the farm," said the pig.

"Oh!" said the rabbit, with a quick little hop. "It would be wonderful to live in a nice house. May I go with you?"

"What can you do to help?" asked the pig.

"I can dig holes for the posts of your house," said the rabbit.

"Oink, oink!" said the pig.

"Baa, baa!" said the sheep.

"Quack, quack!" said the goose.

"That would certainly be a help," said the pig. "Please do come with us."

As the pig and the sheep and the goose and the rabbit walked to the hillside and talked about their new house, they met a rooster.

"Good morning, rooster," said the pig.

"Good morning," replied the rooster. "Where are all of you going this fine morning?"

"We are going to build ourselves a house on the hillside. We all want to live in a nice house," said the pig.

The rooster flapped his wings three times. "Cock-a-doodle-doo!" he crowed. "May I go with you?"

"What can you do to help?" asked the pig.

"I can be your clock," said the rooster. "I will crow every morning and wake you at daybreak."

"Oink, oink!" said the pig.

"Baa, baa!" said the sheep.

"Quack, quack!" said the goose.

And the rabbit gave a little hop.

"That would certainly be a help," said the pig. "Please do come with us."

They all trudged up the hill until they came to a green field. "Oink, oink!" said the pig. "This would be a perfect place to build our house."

"Baa, baa!" said the sheep.

"Quack, quack!" said the goose.

"Cock-a-doodle-do!" said the rooster.

And the rabbit gave a little hop.

So they began to build their house. The pig found the logs for the house. The sheep hauled them together. The rabbit dug the holes for the posts. The goose stuffed moss in the cracks to keep out the rain. And every morning the cock crowed to wake them.

At last the house was built and the cock flew to the very top of the roof and crowed and crowed and crowed.

The Pobble Who Has No Toes

The Pobble who has no toes
   Had once as many as we;
When they said, "Some day you may lose them all,"
   He replied, "Fish fiddle-de-dee!"
And his Aunt Jobiska made him drink
Lavender water tinged with pink,
For she said, "The world in general knows
There's nothing so good for a Pobble's toes!"

The Pobble who has no toes
  Swam across the Bristol Channel;
But before he set out he wrapped his nose
  In a piece of scarlet flannel.
For his Aunt Jobiska said, "No harm
Can come to his toes if his nose is warm;
And it's perfectly known that a Pobble's toes
Are safe—provided he minds his nose."

The Pobble swam fast and well,
  And when boats or ships came near him,
He tinkledy-blinkedy-winkled a bell,
  So that all the world could hear him.
And all the sailors and admirals cried,
When they saw him nearing the further side,
"He has gone to fish for his Aunt Jobiska's
Runcible Cat with crimson whiskers!"

But before he touched the shore—
    The shore of the Bristol Channel—
A sea-green porpoise carried away
    His wrapper of scarlet flannel.
And when he came to observe his feet,
Formerly garnished with toes so neat,
His face at once became forlorn
On perceiving that all his toes were gone!

And nobody ever knew,
    From that dark day to the present,
Whoso had taken the Pobble's toes,
    In a manner so far from pleasant.
Whether the shrimps or crawfish gray,
Or crafty mermaids stole them away—
Nobody knew; and nobody knows
How the Pobble was robbed of his twice five toes!

The Pobble who has no toes
   Was placed in a friendly bark,
And they rowed him back, and carried him up
   To his Aunt Jobiska's park.
And she made him a feast, at his earnest wish,
Of eggs and buttercups fried with fish;
And she said, "It's a fact the whole world knows,
That Pobbles are happier without their toes."

EDWARD LEAR

The Yak

As a friend to the children commend me the Yak
  You will find it exactly the thing:
It will carry and fetch, you can ride on its back,
  Or lead it about with a string.

The Tartar who dwells on the plains of Tibet
  (A desolate region of snow)
Has for centuries made it a nursery pet,
  And surely the Tartar should know!

Then tell your daddy where the Yak can be got,
  And if he is awfully rich
He will buy you the creature—or else he will not.
  (I cannot be positive which.)

HILAIRE BELLOC

CHICKEN LICKEN

ne day when Chicken Licken was scratching among some leaves, an acorn fell out of an oak tree and struck her on the tail.

"Oh," said Chicken Licken, "the sky is falling! I am going to tell the king."

So she set out along the road, walking as fast as she could. To her surprise she met Henny Penny.

"Good morning, Chicken Licken, where are you going?" asked Henny Penny.

"Oh, Henny Penny, the sky is falling and I am going to tell the king!"

"How do you know that the sky is falling?" asked Henny Penny.

"I saw it with my own eyes, I heard it with my own ears, and a piece of it fell on my tail!" said Chicken Licken.

"Then I will go with you," said Henny Penny.

So they set out together, walking as quickly as they could until they met Cocky Locky.

"Good morning, Henny Penny and Chicken Licken," said Cocky Locky. "Where are you going?"

"Oh, Cocky Locky, the sky is falling, and we are going to tell the king!" said Henny Penny.

"How do you know the sky is falling?" asked Cocky Locky.

"Chicken Licken told me," said Henny Penny.

"And I saw it with my own eyes, I heard it with my own ears, and a piece of it fell on my tail!" said Chicken Licken.

"Then I will go with you," said Cocky Locky, "and we will tell the king."

So they walked together, as fast as they could go until they met Ducky Daddles.

"Good morning, Cocky Locky, Henny Penny, and Chicken Licken," said Ducky Daddles. "Where are you going?"

"Oh, Ducky Daddles, the sky is falling and we are going to tell the king!" said Cocky Locky.

"How do you know the sky is falling?" asked Ducky Daddles.

"Henny Penny told me," said Cocky Locky.

"Chicken Licken told me," said Henny Penny.

"And I saw it with my own eyes, I heard it with my own ears, and a piece of it fell on my tail!" said Chicken Licken.

"Then I will go with you," said Ducky Daddles, "and we will tell the king."

So the four of them rushed off together and walked as quickly as they could until they met Goosey Loosey.

"Good morning, Ducky Daddles, Cocky Locky, Henny Penny, and Chicken Licken," said Goosey Loosey. "Where are you going?"

"Oh, Goosey Loosey, the sky is falling and we are going to tell the king!" replied Ducky Daddles.

"How do you know the sky is falling?" asked Goosey Loosey.

"Cocky Locky told me," said Ducky Daddles.

"Henny Penny told me," said Cocky Locky.

"Chicken Licken told me," said Henny Penny.

"And I saw it with my own eyes, I heard it with my own ears, and a piece of it fell on my tail!" said Chicken Licken.

"Then I will go with you," said Goosey Loosey, "and we will tell the king!"

So off they went, walking as fast as they possibly could until they met Turkey Lurkey.

"Good morning, Goosey Loosey, Ducky Daddles, Cocky Locky, Henny Penny, and Chicken Licken," said Turkey Lurkey. "Where are you going?"

"Oh, Turkey Lurkey, the sky is falling and we are going to tell the king!" replied Goosey Loosey.

"How do you know the sky is falling?" asked Turkey Lurkey.

"Ducky Daddles told me," said Goosey Loosey.

"Cocky Locky told me," said Ducky Daddles.

"Henny Penny told me," said Cocky Locky.

"Chicken Licken told me," said Henny Penny.

"And I saw it with my own eyes, I heard it with my own ears, and a piece of it fell on my tail!" said Chicken Licken.

"Then I will go with you," said Turkey Lurkey, "and we will tell the king!"

So they continued on together, walking very quickly until they met Foxy Woxy.

"Good morning, Turkey Lurkey, Goosey Loosey, Ducky Daddles, Cocky Locky, Henny Penny, and Chicken Licken," said Foxy Woxy. "Where are you going?"

"Oh, Foxy Woxy, the sky is falling and we are going to tell the king!" replied Turkey Lurkey.

"How do you know that the sky is falling?" asked Foxy Woxy.

"Goosey Loosey told me," said Turkey Lurkey.

"Ducky Daddles told me," said Goosey Loosey.

"Henny Penny told me," said Cocky Locky.

"Chicken Licken told me," said Henny Penny.

"And I saw it with my own eyes, I heard it with my own ears, and a piece of it fell on my tail," said Chicken Licken.

"Then we will run as fast as we can to my den," said Foxy Woxy, "and then, since I run the fastest of all of us, I will go to tell the king."

So they all ran to Foxy Woxy's den. Those foolish birds never came out again, and the king was never told that the sky was falling.

Farewell to the Farm

The coach is at the door at last;
The eager children, mounting fast
And kissing hands, in chorus sing:
Good-bye, good-bye, to everything!

To house and garden, field and lawn,
The meadow gates we swung upon,
To pump and stable, tree and swing,
Good-bye, good-bye, to everything!

And fare you well for evermore,
Oh ladder at the hayloft door,
Oh hayloft where the cobwebs cling,
Good-bye, good-bye, to everything!

Crack goes the whip, and off we go;
The trees and houses smaller grow;
Last, round the woody turn we swing:
Good-bye, good-bye, to everything!

ROBERT LOUIS STEVENSON

Marching Song

Bring the comb and play upon it!
   Marching, here we come!
Willie cocks his highland bonnet,
   Johnnie beats the drum.

Mary Jane commands the party,
   Peter leads the rear;
Feet in time, alert and hearty,
   Each a Grenadier!

All in the most martial manner
   Marching double-quick;
While the napkin like a banner
   Waves upon the stick!

Here's enough of fame and pillage,
   Great commander Jane!
Now that we've been round the village,
   Let's go home again.

ROBERT LOUIS STEVENSON

The Unseen Playmate

When children are playing alone on the green,
In comes the playmate that never was seen.
When children are happy and lonely and good,
The Friend of the Children comes out of the wood.

Nobody heard him and nobody saw,
His is a picture you never could draw,
But he's sure to be present, abroad or at home,
When children are happy and playing alone.

He lies in the laurels, he runs on the grass,
He sings when you tinkle the musical glass;
Whene'er you are happy and cannot tell why,
The Friend of the Children is sure to be by!

He loves to be little, he hates to be big,
'T is he that inhabits the caves that you dig;
'T is he when you play with your soldiers of tin
That sides with the Frenchmen and never can win.

'T is he, when at night you go off to your bed,
Bids you go to your sleep and not trouble your head;
For wherever they're lying, in cupboard or shelf,
'T is he will take care of your playthings himself!

ROBERT LOUIS STEVENSON

LITTLE TUPPENS

ong, long ago there was a hen who only had one little chicken. The little chicken was named Little Tuppens. One day they went into the woods to look for food. Scratch, scratch, scratch, scratch—all day they were busy among the leaves finding seeds to eat.

"Do not eat the big seeds," said the hen to Little Tuppens. "They will make you choke."

But by and by Little Tuppens found a big seed and ate it. Then Little Tuppens began to choke. This frightened the hen and she ran to the spring as fast as she could go. She said:

> "Please, spring, give me some water.
> Little Tuppens is choking."

The spring replied:

> "Get me a cup and then I will give you some water."

The old hen ran to the oak tree and said:

> "Please, oak tree, give me a cup;
> Then the spring will give me some water.
> Little Tuppens is choking."

The oak tree said:

> "Shake me. Then I will give you a cup."

The hen ran to the little boy and said:

>"Please, little boy, shake the oak tree;
>Then the oak tree will give me a cup;
>And the spring will give me some water.
>Little Tuppens is choking."

The little boy said:

>"Give me some shoes. Then I can shake the oak tree for you."

The hen ran to the shoemaker and said:

>"Please, good shoemaker, give me some shoes for the little boy.
>Then the little boy will shake the oak tree;
>And the oak tree will give me a cup;
>And the spring will give me some water.
>Little Tuppens is choking."

The shoemaker said:

"Get me some leather and then I will make some shoes for the little boy."

The hen ran to the cow and said:

"Please, cow, give me some leather;

Then the shoemaker will make shoes for the little boy;

And the little boy will shake the oak tree;

And the oak tree will give me a cup;

And the spring will give me some water.

Little Tuppens is choking."

The cow said:

"Get me some corn and then I will give you some leather."

The hen ran to the farmer and said:

"Please, good farmer, give me corn for the cow;

Then the cow will give me some leather for the shoemaker;

And the shoemaker will make shoes for the little boy;
And the little boy will shake the oak tree;
And the oak tree will give me a cup;
And the spring will give me some water.
Little Tuppens is choking."
The farmer said:
"Get me a plow and then I can give you some corn."
The hen ran to the blacksmith and said:
"Please, good blacksmith, give me a plow for the farmer;
Then the farmer will give me some corn for the cow;

And the cow will give me some leather for the shoemaker;

And the shoemaker will give me some shoes for the little boy;

And the little boy will shake the oak tree;

And the oak tree will give me a cup;

And the spring will give me some water;

Little Tuppens is choking."

The blacksmith said:

"Get me some iron and then I can give you a plow."

The hen ran to the dwarfs, who were miners, and asked for some iron for the blacksmith.

When she had told her story about Little Tuppens to the dwarfs, they wanted to help. They quickly went into their cave and brought out some iron for the blacksmith.

Then the blacksmith made a plow for the farmer;
And the farmer gave the hen some corn for the cow;
And the cow gave her some leather for the shoemaker;
And the shoemaker made some shoes for the little boy;
And the little boy shook the oak tree;
And the oak tree gave the old hen a cup;
And the spring gave her some water;
And the hen gave the water to Little Tuppens;
And Little Tuppens stopped choking.

Playgrounds

In summer I am very glad
   We children are so small,
For we can see a thousand things
   That men can't see at all.

They don't know much about the moss
   And all the stones they pass:
They never lie and play among
   The forests in the grass:

They walk about a long way off;
   And when we're at the sea,
Let father stoop as best he can
   He can't find things like me.

But, when the snow is on the ground
   And all the puddles freeze,
I wish that I were very tall,
   High up above the trees.

LAURENCE ALMA-TADEMA

The Way for Billy and Me

Where the pools are bright and deep,
Where the gray trout lies asleep,
Up the river and over the lea,
That's the way for Billy and me.

Where the blackbird sings the latest,
Where the hawthorn blooms the sweetest,
Where the nestlings chirp and flee,
That's the way for Billy and me.

Where the mowers mow the cleanest,
Where the hay lies thick and greenest;
There to track the homeward bee,
That's the way for Billy and me.

Where the hazel bank is steepest,
Where the shadow falls the deepest,
Where the clustering nuts fall free,
That's the way for Billy and me.

Why the boys should drive away
Little sweet maidens from the play,
Or love to banter and fight so well,
That's the thing I never could tell.

But this I know, I love to play
Through the meadow, among the hay;
Up the water and over the lea,
That's the way for Billy and me.

JAMES HOGG

Looking-Glass River

Smooth it glides upon its travel,
Here a wimple, there a gleam—
    O the clean gravel!
    O the smooth stream!

Sailing blossoms, silver fishes,
Paven pools as clear as air—
    How a child wishes
    To live down there!

We can see our colored faces
Floating on the shaken pool
    Down in cool places,
    Dim and very cool.

Till a wind or water wrinkle,
Dipping marten, plumping trout,
    Spreads in a twinkle
    And blots all out.

See the rings pursue each other;
All below grows black as night,
    Just as if Mother
    Had blown out the light!

Patience, children, just a minute—
See the spreading circles die;
    The stream and all in it
    Will clear by-and-by.

ROBERT LOUIS STEVENSON

The Old Man Who Said Hush!

There was an Old Man who said, "Hush!
I perceive a young bird in this bush!"
    When they said, "Is it small?"
    He replied, "Not at all!
It is four times as big as the bush!"

The Old Man With a Beard

There was an Old Man with a beard,
Who said, "It is just as I feared!
    Two Owls and a Hen,
    Four Larks and a Wren,
Have all built their nests in my beard!"

EDWARD LEAR

The Hayloft

Through all the pleasant meadow side
The grass grew shoulder-high,
Till the shining scythes went far and wide
And cut it down to dry.

Those green and sweetly smelling crops
They led in wagons home;
And they piled them here in mountaintops
For mountaineers to roam.

Here is Mount Clear, Mount Rusty Nail,
Mount Eagle, and Mount High;
The mice that in these mountains dwell,
No happier are than I!

Oh, what a joy to clamber there,
Oh, what a place for play,
With the sweet, the dim, the dusty air,
The happy hills of hay!

ROBERT LOUIS STEVENSON

75

The GINGERBREAD BOY

long, long time ago there was a little old woman and a little old man who lived in a little cottage. They had no children, although they had always wanted at least one.

On a bright, sunny morning the woman said to her husband, "I think I will make us a nice gingerbread boy."

"That's a silly idea," said the man, laughing.

The woman paid no attention to his laughter as she took all the ingredients out of the cupboard. Then she measured and mixed until she had a smooth ball of spicy brown dough. Humming a little tune, she rolled out the dough with her wooden rolling pin. When the dough was all the same thickness she carefully cut out the shape of a gingerbread boy. She used plump raisins to make his eyes. For his smiling mouth she used little cinnamon candies. She made his buttons with tiny raisins. Then she stood back and admired her work.

"What a lovely gingerbread boy you are," she said.

She carefully slid the gingerbread boy onto a baking tray. Then she popped it into the oven. Before long the kitchen was filled with the delicious smell of gingerbread.

When the woman thought that the gingerbread boy was nicely baked, she gently opened the oven door and pulled out the baking tray.

To her great surprise, the gingerbread boy stood up and then jumped off the baking tray, ran across the kitchen, through the open door, and down the path in front of the house.

The woman was amazed to see her gingerbread boy running away. "Come back! Oh, please come back!" she called.

But the gingerbread boy laughed and just kept running, and the woman ran after him.

They soon passed the old man, who was sitting in the shade reading a book. He threw down his book and joined in the chase. But the gingerbread boy did not slow down. He ran and he ran and he ran. And the little old woman and the little old man ran after him.

As the gingerbread boy ran on he passed a big dog. The dog began to bark. The gingerbread boy laughed and called out:

> *I am a gingerbread boy, I am, I am.*
> *I ran away from the little old woman,*
> *I ran away from the little old man,*
> *I can run away from you, I can, I can.*

The gingerbread boy ran on and on. And behind him ran the dog, the little old man, and the little old woman.

It wasn't long before the gingerbread boy passed a cat.

"Stop, stop," called the cat.

The gingerbread boy wouldn't stop. He didn't even slow down. He just laughed merrily and called out:

I am a gingerbread boy, I am, I am.
I ran away from the little old woman,
I ran away from the little old man,
I ran away from the dog,
I can certainly run away from you, I can, I can.

The gingerbread boy ran on and on. And behind him ran the cat, the dog, the little old man, and, of course, the little old woman.

By and by he passed a farmyard where there was a big pig. "Stop, stop!" called the pig. "I'd like a little bite of you. I know you'd taste better than the slops I eat."

The gingerbread boy didn't stop. He just ran faster and called back:

> *I am a gingerbread boy, I am, I am.*
> *I ran away from the little old woman,*
> *I ran away from the little old man,*
> *I ran away from the dog,*
> *I ran away from the cat,*
> *I can run away from you, too, I can, I can.*

So the gingerbread boy ran and ran, and the pig ran after him just as fast as his short legs would go. And behind the pig ran the cat, the dog, the little old man, and the little old woman.

The gingerbread boy continued running, and soon the path turned and he was running alongside a river. There the gingerbread boy ran past a boy who was fishing. The real boy was so surprised to see a boy made of gingerbread that he yelled, "Please stop! I want to talk to you. I've never before seen a boy made of gingerbread who could run, or could even walk."

But the gingerbread boy laughed and yelled back:

I am a gingerbread boy, I am, I am.
I ran away from the little old woman,
I ran away from the little old man,
I ran away from the dog,
I ran away from the cat,
I ran away from the pig,
I can run away from you, I can, I can.

The gingerbread boy ran and ran, and the boy ran after him, carrying his fishing rod. And behind the boy ran the pig, the cat, the dog, the little old man, and the little old woman.

By and by the path ran up a hill. As the gingerbread boy was approaching the top of the hill, he saw a fox slink out of the bushes. He laughed and called up to the fox:

I am a gingerbread boy, I am, I am.
I ran away from the little old woman,
I ran away from the little old man,
I ran away from the dog,
I ran away from the cat,
I ran away from the pig,
I ran away from the boy,
I can run away from you, I can, I can.

The fox called back:

> *You ran away from the little old woman,*
>
> *You ran away from the little old man,*
>
> *You ran away from the dog,*
>
> *You ran away from the cat,*
>
> *You ran away from the pig,*
>
> *You ran away from the boy,*
>
> *But you cannot run away from me.*

And as the gingerbread boy passed him, the fox reached out and snapped him up in his sharp teeth, and that was the end of the gingerbread boy.

And this is the end of the story.

Young Night Thought

All night long and every night,
When my mama puts out the light,
I see the people marching by,
As plain as day, before my eye.

Armies and emperors and kings,
All carrying different kinds of things,
And marching in so grand a way,
You never saw the like by day.

So fine a show was never seen
At the great circus on the green;
For every kind of beast and man
Is marching in that caravan.

At first they move a little slow,
But still the faster on they go,
And still beside them close I keep
Until we reach the town of Sleep.

ROBERT LOUIS STEVENSON

The Moon

The moon has a face like the clock in the hall;
She shines on thieves on the garden wall,
On streets and fields and harbor quays,
And birdies asleep in the forks of the trees.

The squalling cat and the squeaking mouse,
The howling dog by the door of the house,
The bat that lies in bed at noon,
All love to be out by the light of the moon.

But all of the things that belong to the day
Cuddle to sleep to be out of her way;
And flowers and children close their eyes
Till up in the morning the sun shall arise.

ROBERT LOUIS STEVENSON

Wynken, Blynken, and Nod

Wynken, Blynken, and Nod one night
   Sailed off in a wooden shoe—
Sailed on a river of crystal light,
   Into a sea of dew.
"Where are you going, and what do you wish?"
   The old moon asked the three.
"We have come to fish for the herring-fish
   That live in this beautiful sea;
Nets of silver and gold have we!"
   Said Wynken, Blynken, and Nod.

The old moon laughed and sang a song,
   As they rocked in the wooden shoe,
And the wind that sped them all night long,
   Ruffled the waves of dew.

The little stars were the herring-fish
    That lived in that beautiful sea—
"Now cast your nets wherever you wish—
    But never afeard are we";
So cried the stars to the fishermen three:
    Wynken, Blynken, and Nod.

All night long their nets they threw
    For the fish in the twinkling foam—
Then down from the sky came the wooden shoe,
    Bringing the fishermen home;
'Twas all so pretty a sail, it seemed
    As if it could not be;
And some folks thought 'twas a dream they'd dreamed
    Of sailing that beautiful sea—
But I shall name you the fishermen three:
    Wynken, Blynken, and Nod.

Wynken and Blynken are two little eyes,
    And Nod is a little head,
And the wooden shoe that sailed the skies
    Is a wee one's trundle bed.
So shut your eyes while mother sings
    Of wonderful sights that be,
And you shall see the beautiful things
    As you rock in the misty sea,
Where the old shoe rocked the fishermen three:
    Wynken, Blynken, and Nod.

EUGENE FIELD

Windy Nights

Whenever the moon and stars are set,
   Whenever the wind is high,
All night long in the dark and wet,
   A man goes riding by.
Late in the night when the fires are out,
Why does he gallop and gallop about?

Whenever the trees are crying aloud,
   And ships are tossed at sea,
By, on the highway, low and loud,
   By, at the gallop goes he.
By at the gallop he goes, and then
By he comes back at the gallop again.

ROBERT LOUIS STEVENSON